More of
Grandfather's Stories From Viet Nam

Written by Donna Roland
Illustrations by Kevin Rones

ISBN 0-941996-12-3
Copyright © 1985
OPEN MY WORLD PUBLISHING
1300 Lorna St., El Cajon, CA 92020

Meet Vinh and Lang. They live in America with their mother and father, and their grandfather.

Vinh and Lang's family came to America from a small, far away country called South Viet Nam.

Almost every night after dinner Grandfather tells Vinh and Lang stories about their homeland. One of the stories that they like the best is the story about the lizard and Vu Cong Due.

Many years ago there was a poor farmer and his wife who worked very hard. They had one young son whose name was Vu Cong Due.

Due's mother and father worked all day in the fields. In the evenings they worked other jobs. Their dream was to save enough money to buy the land they lived and worked on.

But even with all their hard work, there never seemed to be enough money left to save any. So they decided to borrow the money from the richest man in their village.

The rich man agreed to loan Due's
family the money. They agreed to pay
him back more than they borrowed,
but the land would finally be theirs.
Due's family worked even harder,
everyone had many jobs.

Due had to pack and sweep their
dirt floor, and was in charge of caring
for the beets and cabbage plants.
He also had to get fresh water from
the stream.

But no matter how hard they worked, there was still just enough money to buy what they needed. Then the day came when the rich man was to be paid back.

When he came to Due's house to get
his money he found no one there but
young Due. "Where are your mother
and father?," asked the rich man.

"They are not home. They are working,"
answered Due. "Where are they
working?," questioned the man. Due
answered by saying, "My father has
gone to cut down living trees and
plant dead ones."

"My mother is in the marketplace
selling the wind and buying the moon."
"What!," cried the rich man. And he
asked the same question again.

The rich man asked again and
again but Due's answer was always
the same. "I came here today to
get my money." said the rich man,

"but if you will tell me where your mother and father *really* are, I will forget about the money they owe me." Of course he did not mean what he said.

The man thought this would make
Due tell him what his riddle meant so
he could find out where the boy's
parents really were.

"Are you willing to say your offer again
in front of someone else?" asked
Due. The rich man looked around
and seeing no one else was there
he said, "Of course."

Due looked around and said, "There, there is our witness." pointing to Thach Sung, a lizard who was resting on one of the bamboo poles. The rich man made his offer again.

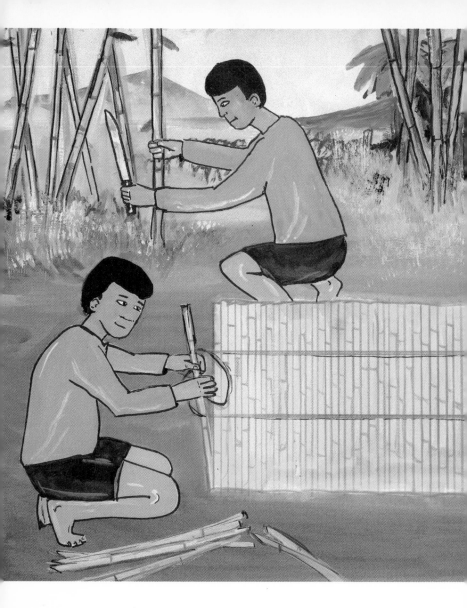

Due then explained where his mother and father were. "When my father goes out to cut down living trees and plant dead ones, he is cutting bamboo and making them into a fence."

When my mother is in the marketplace
selling the wind and buying the
moon, she is selling fans so that she
can buy oil for our lamps."

After hearing Due's answers the rich man left. Due could not wait to share the good news with his mother and father. But the next night the rich man came back and wanted his money.

Forgetting all about his offer to forget about the loan, he brought with him the Mandarin, who was the judge for the village. The Mandarin asked Due to tell his side of the story.

Due told him and said he even had a witness. "Who else heard the offer?" asked the Mandarin. "Thach Sung, our lizard who was on the stove at the time," said young Due.

But before the Mandarin could ask
anything else the rich many cried out,
"That's not true! He was not on the
stove, he was on a bamboo pole."
"So there *was* a witness and you *did*
make the offer," said the Mandarin.

"The boy's family does not have to pay you because in our country a person's word is always good, and it is right to do what you have said you will do."

Due's family did pay the money back when they could. And the rich man learned his lesson, and began treating others the way he wanted to be treated. Just like Grandfather wants Vinh and Lang to do.